I AM ANNA

By Christy Webster
Illustrated by Alan Batson

A GOLDEN BOOK • NEW YORK

Copyright © 2020 Disney Enterprises, Inc. All rights reserved. Published by Golden
Books, an imprint of Random House Children's Books, a division of Penguin Random
House LLC, 1745 Broadway, New York, NY 10019, and in Canada by Penguin Random
House Canada Limited, Toronto. Golden Books, A Golden Book, A Little Golden Book,
the G colophon, and the distinctive gold spine are registered trademarks of Penguin
Random House LLC.
rhcbooks.com
ISBN 978-0-7364-4018-9 (trade) — ISBN 978-0-7364-4019-6 (ebook)
Printed in the United States of America
10 9 8 7 6 5 4 3 2 1

I am ANNA.

I live in the
kingdom of
ARENDELLE.

My sister, Elsa, and I were really close when we were little.

We built a snowman.

We went sledding.

We skated on the pond.

But one day she just shut me out, and I didn't know why.

I spent my days
talking to paintings.

It was lonely.

But then I found someone special.

Elsa wouldn't bless my marriage
to Hans because we'd just met . . .

that day.

I got mad,

she got upset . . . .

. . . and her magic accidentally froze our **kingdom**!

She RAN AWAY.

I had to find her. I knew my sister
wouldn't hurt me.
And I was *born* ready for adventure.

On my search, I met new friends—Kristoff, Sven, and Olaf!

I found Elsa
on the North Mountain.

But she wanted to be alone.

Elsa didn't mean to do it,
but her magic froze my heart!

Kristoff took me to see the trolls.

They told me that only an act of
true love can thaw a frozen heart.

We raced back to Hans.

But I was
wrong about him.
It wasn't true
love.

Olaf helped me understand
what true *love* is.

I *love* my sister.

And my act of
love for her thawed
my heart.

As Olaf says . . . some people
are worth **melting** for.